TILLY and MILLY

Kate Summers

ILLUSTRATED BY
Maggie Kneen

Orion
Children's Books

First published in Great Britain in 1998
by Orion Children's Books
a division of the Orion Publishing Group Ltd
Orion House
5 Upper St Martin's Lane
London WC2H 9EA

Printed and bound in India

Tilly was a mouse who lived in the country.
She was every bit a country mouse,
from her ears

to the tip of her tail.

Only the sharpest eyes could have seen where
she lived —

down a lane,

by the meadow,

in tree roots under a hedge.

Tilly was poor, but she worked hard to make her home comfortable. Each room was as neat as two pins, with everything a simple mouse could want: a table, some chairs and a soft little bed — with a quilt she had sewn, stitch by stitch.

Every day Tilly got up early, and did all her
mousework before breakfast. She plumped up the
cushions, swept the floor and even polished the
stove.

Tilly spent most of her days gathering food.
It wasn't always easy finding enough to eat,
but at harvest time there was plenty.

She picked corn from the fields,

cherries from the orchard and . . .

nuts along the hedgerow.

And because she was a sensible mouse, Tilly filled her larder with all these good things, and stored them up for winter.

One sunny morning Tilly
had been out collecting
acorns. She had just
returned when the postman
arrived with a letter.
It was from her friend
Milly, who lived in town.
She read:

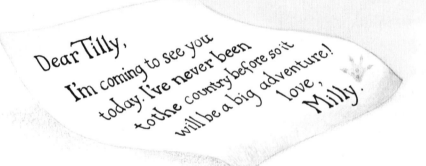

Dear Tilly,
I'm coming to see you
today. I've never been
to the country before so it
will be a big adventure!
love,
Milly.

Tilly was so excited, she hugged the postman!
She told him all about her friend.
"Well, I hope you've got enough food," said the
postman. "I've heard town mice eat a lot."

When the postman had gone, Tilly put on her apron and began cooking straight away. She was a good cook, and soon there was a delicious smell of baking coming from the kitchen.

After that Tilly dusted
the furniture again
(she had already done it once)
and waited for Milly to arrive.

While she was waiting, Tilly began to worry.
She worried about what they would do all day.
Milly had often written and told her about life in
town. It sounded much more exciting than her
own. I hope she won't be bored, thought Tilly
anxiously.

The clock ticked away.
One hour. Two hours.

Meanwhile Tilly kept peeping through her
window, and hoped Milly hadn't got lost.
As the clock struck six, she heard
a knock at the door . . .
and there was her friend
on the doorstep.

The mice kissed noses.

"At last!" squeaked Tilly. "I thought you'd never come."

"I would have been here sooner," explained Milly, "only a snail kindly carried my bags, and it has taken us all day!"

Milly was hungry after her journey, so the two mice sat down to supper. They ate:

cabbage soup

pickled chestnuts

nut pasties

and

bread

seedcake

plum dumplings

and hot apple pie

Milly had a big appetite and finished every crumb.
"Do you have any cheese?" she asked hopefully.
"I'm afraid not," said Tilly.
Oh dear, no cheese! thought Milly.
But she was far too polite to complain.

That evening the two friends sat talking until bedtime. Then, since Tilly had thoughtfully given Milly her bed,

she curled up in a chair.

Milly lay awake for a long time. It was so quiet in
the country, she couldn't sleep a wink.

At dawn, when she
was sound asleep,
the birds woke her up
with their singing.

After breakfast the two mice went to the meadow
to pick flowers. Tilly was going to show Milly
how to make summer wine.
"We'll need a bunch of buttercups, and lots of
daisies," she said.

While they were busy, a bee came along.
It buzzed all round Milly's head.

Bzzz!

Bzzz!

Milly had never seen a bee before.
"Go away!" she squealed. And ran.

Another day they went walking near the farm.
Suddenly a sheep put its head through the fence
and went

Baa!

It frightened Milly to pieces!

Well, Tilly tried her best to make her friend happy. But what with one thing and another, Milly decided to go back home.

"Come with me," she said. "I live in a big house. We'll have scrumptious meals every day. You'll love it!"

Now Tilly had always wanted
to see where Milly lived.
So she put on her very best
hat, and went to town.

The two mice walked through the fields and
over the hills.

The sun went down and the moon came up.

At last the friends reached town.

They scurried along a busy street,

until Milly stopped outside a house.
"In here," she said,
disappearing through
a hole in the wall.

Tilly followed. It was all so strange, she felt just
a little nervous.

Milly led the way along
a hall. The carpet tickled
their feet.

Then down a winding
staircase. Down round,
and down again to a room
at the very bottom.

And there in a corner stood
a doll's house. It had painted
windows, a roof and chimney,
and a proper front door with
a bell.
"We're home," said Milly.
"Step inside."

Milly showed Tilly all round her house.
There were lots of rooms, and each one was
beautifully furnished.
There was a green room for sitting in;
a red room with a dining table,
and a blue room for afternoon tea.
Tilly peeped into the kitchen. It was full of
wonderful things; tiny pots, pans, spoons and
dishes – everything a mouse cook could want.
And best of all was a shiny new stove
(the latest in town)
with knobs you
could turn,
on and off.

Then they went upstairs.
"This is your room, Tilly," said Milly. "I hope you like it."
It was primrose yellow, with curtains to match, tied with tassels and bows.
"Oh!" sighed Tilly. "How lovely."

There was a feather bed with lacy pillows, a dressing-table and stool. The wallpaper was printed with daisies, and made Tilly think of home. Tilly peered into every nook and cupboard, squealing with delight.

"Time to eat," said Milly at last.
"My tummy is grumbling."

Tilly thought they would be going to the kitchen,
but Milly laughed.
"I don't cook at all," she said.
"There's always food in the
Big House."
So the two friends scampered out of the doll's
house in search of supper. They went all the way
upstairs to the Big Kitchen . . .

and into the larder.

"Here, give me your paw," said Milly
as they clambered on to a shelf.

Tilly gasped to see so much food. There were:

chocolate cakes,

currant buns,

crusty pies and

biscuits;

jars of jam,

a tray of tarts and . . .

enormous chunks of CHEESE!

"Tuck in," said Milly. "Have as much as you like."

But before they could nibble anything,
a CAT came along,

jumped on a chair and . . .

SPRANG!
The two mice leapt for their lives! They scuttled
along a skirtingboard – the cat just a whisker behind.

"Help! Help!" squealed Tilly,
running like the wind.
"Faster!" squeaked Milly,
racing down a passage.

The cat pounced
and chased them
all the way back
to the doll's house.
But he couldn't get in.

When they were safe inside Milly tried to comfort her friend.

"You mustn't mind that old cat," she said. "He often tries to catch me, but I'm far too quick for him.'

"Well, cat and mouse games are not for me," sniffed Tilly, who had begun to cry. "It's all very well living in this fine house. But in my little home in the country, I enjoy my meals in peace!" Milly had to agree.

"I risk getting caught every day," she said.

"But town life suits me best."

So the next morning, when the cat had gone, the two mice said goodbye.

"Write soon," said Tilly.
"I will," said Milly.
"We'll always stay
good friends."

Then Tilly ran back to the country, and settled down in her favourite chair.